To you, dear reader: a welcome to the countryside

M. J. R.

To my parents, who took me on many family drives,
and my wife, Janice, who joins me on them still

M. B.

Text copyright © 2007 by Michael J. Rosen
Illustrations copyright © 2007 by Marc Burckhardt

First edition 2007

Library of Congress Cataloging-in-Publication Data
Rosen, Michael J., date.
A drive in the country / by Michael J. Rosen ; illustrated by Marc Burckhardt. — 1st ed.
p. cm.
Summary: Relates the adventures of a family and their dog on a Sunday drive to the country.
ISBN 978-0-7636-2140-7
[1. Automobile travel — Fiction. 2. Country life — Fiction. 3. Family life — Fiction.]
I. Burckhardt, Marc, date, ill. II. Title.
PZ7.R71868Dri 2007
[Fic] — dc22   2006051834

2 4 6 8 10 9 7 5 3 1

Printed in Singapore

This book was typeset in OPTI-Action Brush.
The illustrations were done in acrylic on board.

Candlewick Press
2067 Massachusetts Avenue
Cambridge, Massachusetts 02140

visit us at www.candlewick.com

A DRIVE in the COUNTRY

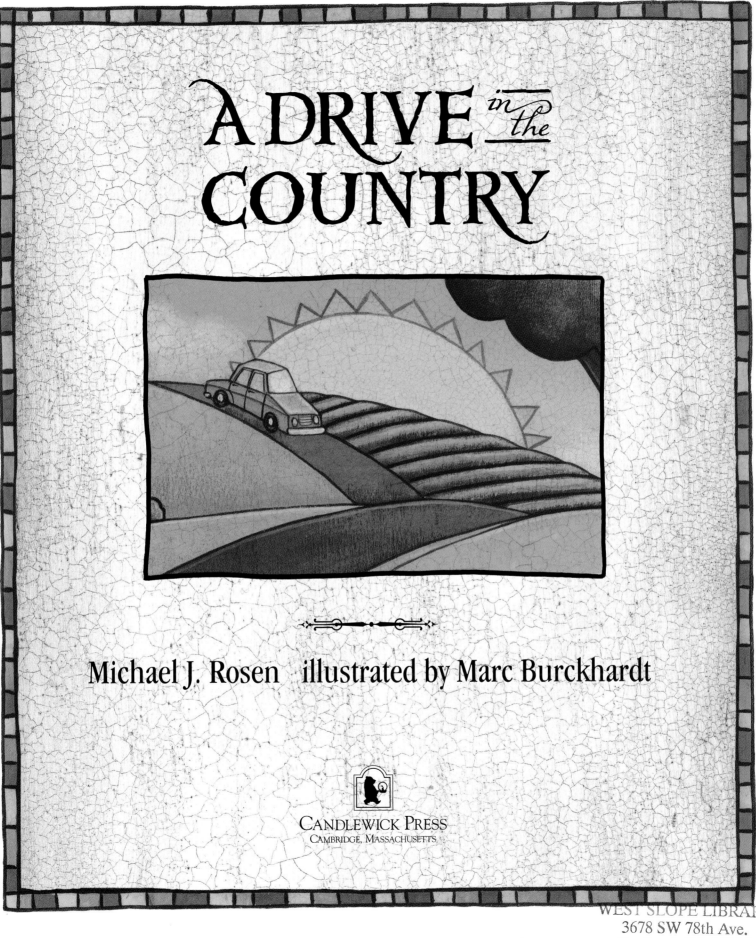

Michael J. Rosen   illustrated by Marc Burckhardt

CANDLEWICK PRESS
CAMBRIDGE, MASSACHUSETTS

SUNDAY MORNING! We're driving to the country!
All five of us and our basset hound, Shirley
(she makes six); we load up the car for adventure.
My mom fills the cooler with drinks and snacks.
We cram our backpacks with playing cards and jars
for keeping unusual bugs and Shirley's treats,
and spending money, puzzle books, and comics.

And now we're off! On a road that Dad insists
stretches clear across the country like the crack
in the salt map I mixed last year at school.

We have no destination (at least, Dad
won't say just where we're going), no reason to be home
for supper, no place we need to reach by dark on the map that's as big
as a baby blanket spread across our laps.
(Mom refolds its zillion folds for us.)

But better than anywhere we end up
are all the roads that take us wherever and back:
twisting skinny roads with dips and bumps
that make my stomach flip, with smells of hay
and poop from pigs and that steamy scent
of sprinkled rain on sun-baked roads—and *skunks*!

I like the yellow lines disappearing
just at the top of a hill, as if our car
were lifting off instead of coasting down.
I still can't figure out those slicks of water
up ahead and how they just . . . vanish.

Today we're lucky. We find a lake with ducks
to feed our pretzels and peanuts (look, they sink!).
Then Shirley gets to chase a pair of mallards
swimming around some kids in a paddleboat
that could have been us, since sometimes we rent one—
or a rowboat to fish for bluegill and perch.

At the shallow end,
there's a place to wade barefoot
and balance on the slipperiest rocks.
Under one, I catch a crawdad sleeping,
and hold him while he waves
his pincher hello at my sister,
who screams like she's afraid (she's not).
Schools of minnows race between my legs.

And at the farthest end,
there's a waterfall
with a room behind
the shooshing water.
We sneak inside and gaze out
through the blurry wall.

Guess what we find at this fruit stand? *Yellow*
watermelons and splotched and spotty gourds
and milk-and-sugar corn in the bed of a truck.
Then we poke inside its tiny store
that's got only one or two of anything
on the wooden shelves, *plus* night crawlers
and arrowheads for sale, and frosted doughnuts,
licorice, and jelly made from roses—really!—
and jars of piccalilli (whatever that is)
and a large-mouth bass yawning on the wall.

Then the scenery's just field after field,

so with my folded-paper fortuneteller

I predict a few things, but then Dad

decides it's Joke Time (he never forgets

a single one he's heard!), while my sister

pretends she knows some jokes too and reads

STORE

to see who can find the town with the stupidest name . . .

and I open the map

and my little brother

— like Millieville and Sludge and Old Peru.

some silly riddles from a library book

Since no one's found this road but us, we comb
the berm for buckeyes with their spiny shells,
or hickory nuts, or black walnuts that stain
our fingers yellow, or Osage oranges huge
and pimply as grapefruits, or leaves turning so ruby
bright or purple-edged we have to mail them
to our cousins who don't have autumn where they live.

Instead, we spot some milkweed entwined
around a fence, its pods about to split.
We pluck as many as we can cradle in the
stretched-out hems of our shirts and head for the car.
We split the pods with their million airy seeds,
and send them out the window of the speeding car,
one pod at a time, in a stream of wishes.

We pass a bunch of barns. Old ones are best,
barns that just collapsed, or barns painted
HOPEWELL DAIRY FARM with roofs like a giant
fish's scales, or barns with flocks of lambs
or black-faced sheep and mammoth spirals of hay
that look like alien cocoons that dropped to Earth.

Dad pulls over so we can feed some horses.
"Hey, Mom," my sister asks, "did you remember
the sugar cubes?" "I have some Sweet'n Low,"
Mom jokes, fishing a packet from her purse.
She does have treats for the horse, and we take turns
patting its muzzle, which is softer than Shirley's ears.

My sister starts a game of License Plates
(we've never spotted Hawaii or Idaho),
and then I Spy, while my brother counts
Volkswagen Bugs and pesters Dad,

HAWAII
ALO-HA

POTA-TO
· IDAHO ·

"Let's stop for root-beer floats somewhere.
Come on!"

It's dark enough to watch for burned-out headlights,
which Mom says means you have to kiss your neighbor.
We keep a lookout for graveyards, too, because then
you have to lift both feet off the floor
and hold your breath—even Dad does!—
until we've passed it, because . . . because you do!

And now it's sprinkling, so Mom begins to sing,
"It's raining, it's pouring . . ." and we all start shouting
above the *thwack-thwack* of the wiper blades:
"I've been working on the railroad . . ." and "Oh,
my darling, Clementine," and lots of tunes
whose words we can't remember. And then, it's weird:

but even with everyone talking loud above
the radio turned up louder since the wind's
whipping over the car, and even with the loud
city sounds and traffic honking again,
I fall asleep—I do!—on our ride home.

But since I don't wake up, Mom and Dad,
they let me sleep, so that later, in the car
parked beside a lamppost, all by myself,
I open my eyes and take a whole minute
to figure out where I am, and that this
is our car, and that right here is where I live,
and that wherever in the world we've been
today, the only place we wanted to go
was Together, just our family,
and a Sunday drive in the country took us there.